Arkansas

Shreveport

cotton

natural gas

soybeans

cotton

Louisiana

lumber

N

Red River

Texas

Sabine River

cattle

pecans

Mississippi River

Mississippi

fruit

cotton

Baton Rouge

Lake Pontchartrain

sheep

sweet potatoes

Atchafalaya River

Mississippi River

rice

petroleum

salt

New Orleans

oysters

sugar cane

catfish

shrimp crayfish

Baratari Bay

Gulf of Mexico

The Twelve Days of Christmas in Louisiana

by Jean Cassels

illustrated by
Lynne Avril

STERLING CHILDREN'S BOOKS
New York

Dear Paul,

Surprise! I'm sending you a ticket to come visit us for the twelve days of Christmas! This is a special time in Louisiana. Christmas doesn't really end until Twelfth Night (January 6th here in New Orleans). That's when Dad and I always take down the tree. And Twelfth Night is the start of Carnival, with really fun parades and costumes.

This is my favorite time of year—with Christmas lights sparkling in the trees at night and decorations everywhere. And even though it's winter, there are still lots of pretty flowers, especially pansies in purple, gold, and green, the colors of Mardi Gras.

Dad and I have a lot of fun things planned for when you get here and some surprises, too. I think you're going to have a great time!

See you soon!
Your cousin, Rosalie

December 26th

Dear Mom and Dad,

Hello from Louisiana! Lots of people here are celebrating the first day of Christmas. Rosalie says the fun is just beginning. This morning Uncle Joe drove us across the longest highway over water in the world! The Causeway Bridge is 24 miles long and goes right across Lake Pontchartrain. When we got to the other side, we explored the Tchefuncte River. I saw my first bald cypress tree— did you know it's the Louisiana state tree? Bald cypresses are funny-looking because they have knees—lots of pointy, knobby parts that stick up out of the ground and the water. Rosalie says the trees breathe through their knees!

We also saw a bunch of pelicans. (The brown pelican is the official state bird.) Uncle Joe recited this funny poem:

"A wonderful bird is the pelican;
Its beak can hold more than its belly can."

Hard to believe, but Rosalie swears it's true: a pelican's beak can hold almost three gallons of fish!

Love,
Paul

December 27th

Dear Mom and Dad,

Today we went to the special swamp exhibit at the Audubon Zoo to see Spots, a huge white alligator with blue eyes. The zookeeper said that he isn't an albino alligator, because if he were, his eyes would be PINK. Weird!

In the 1980s, alligators in Louisiana almost disappeared because of hunters and predators! So a team of researchers took alligator babies from the wild and raised them in special ponds in a marsh where they were safe. They planned to release them back into the wild when the gators grew up. When the researchers went to check on the gator nests in the marsh, they found that 18 white baby alligators had hatched in one nest! Spots is one of those. If you see a white alligator in any other zoo, it's probably one of Spots' cousins!

Love,
Paul

December 28th

Dear Mom and Dad,

Rosalie gave me three quacking marsh ducks today! We all went to the White Kitchen Eagle Preserve, where a boardwalk leads from the highway right into the marsh. Uncle Joe says that the marshes and other waterways have really begun to recover from the damage caused by Hurricane Katrina. Rosalie brought her binoculars and I spotted two bald eagles! Winter is the best time to see them since they're here to mate and raise their babies.

There were lots and lots of birds flying over the marsh. Uncle Joe says ducks and songbirds from all over the country migrate south to Louisiana in the winter. Some of the birds are on their way to Central and South America. They use the marshes as their rest stop so they can get plenty to eat before they fly all that way. There are many other critters in the marsh, too. We saw an otter, some turtles, and a big frog!

Love,
Paul

On the third day of Christmas,
my cousin gave to me...

3 marsh ducks

2 baby gators,
and a pelican in a cypress tree.

December 29th

Dear Mom and Dad,

Today I saw the Mississippi River for the very first time. I even took a cruise on a big old riverboat.

I heard the captain say that the river is more than 2,000 miles long, starting in Minnesota and ending here at the Gulf of Mexico. I raced Rosalie to the upper deck to get a good view of the huge oil tankers, barges, and little tugboats. Uncle Joe told us that New Orleans is a major port city—the port was as busy as a highway! I also learned that all of Louisiana used to belong to France, but in 1803 it was sold to the Americans as part of the Louisiana Purchase. If that hadn't happened, everyone would be speaking French down here!

Love,
Paul

P.S. Out on the Mississippi River, I felt like Huckleberry Finn.

December 30th

Dear Mom and Dad,

In Jackson Square today we listened to an amazing jazz band. Uncle Joe kept saying, "Those cats are swingin'!" They led us down Esplanade Avenue, second-line dancing and high-stepping all the way to the Louisiana State Museum and the Historical Jazz Collection. We got to see lots of cool photos and musical instruments. Rosalie even picked out some recordings by famous musicians for me to hear: Louis Armstrong, Jelly Roll Morton, and Joe "King" Oliver. Those cats were swingin', too!

In the mid 1890s, there were three kinds of music being played in New Orleans. Swinging ragtime came from the Midwest, and African-Americans brought blues and gospel music from the Mississippi Delta. African-American and Creole musicians played together and mixed all that music to make something brand new called jazz. When I get home, I want to learn how to play the trumpet!

Love,
Paul

December 31st

Dear Mom and Dad,

Today we went on a ghost hunt at one of the most haunted of all haunted houses, the Myrtles Plantation in St. Francisville. Rosalie spotted six ghosts . . . Boo!

A lot of people used to work in the cotton fields around the big, fancy house. The mansion was so cool and really old—it was built in 1796. One rumor says that it was built on top of an ancient Native American burial ground and that's why it's so haunted! Also, lots of people died here of yellow fever, and the tour guide said that their ghosts—and many others—are still haunting the grounds. There's even one ghost of a girl who shows up right before thunderstorms. Spooky!

Tonight we're going back to Jackson Square in New Orleans for the New Year's Eve party. Rosalie says there will be lots of music and the countdown to midnight. Then we'll watch the fireworks over the Mississippi! Happy New Year!!

Love,
Paul

January 1st

Dear Mom and Dad,

Rosalie gave me a map today marked with red Xs where seven of pirate Jean Lafitte's buried treasures might be. Uncle Joe says that there could be millions of dollars in gold and silver buried in Barataria Bay! Wouldn't it be great if Jean Lafitte could show Rosalie and me where he hid his treasure?

Remember when I did my class project on the Battle of New Orleans that ended the War of 1812? Well, today we walked across the Chalmette Battlefield, where it took place. In 1814, when the British were planning to attack America, they offered Jean Lafitte a full pardon for his attack on British ships if he would help them. (They knew he had lots of men, boats, guns, and ammunition.) Jean Lafitte decided to help the Americans instead. With his help, America won the battle and saved New Orleans. Hooray for Jean Lafitte!

Love,
Paul

On the seventh day of Christmas,
my cousin gave to me...

7 secret treasures

6 ghosts a-spooking, 5 golden horns,
4 riverboats, 3 marsh ducks, 2 baby gators,
and a pelican in a cypress tree.

January 2nd

Dear Mom and Dad,

Rosalie gave me eight bottles of Louisiana hot sauce . . . . and wow, is it HOT!

Today we went to Avery Island to tour the Tabasco factory. That's where the world-famous hot pepper sauce with the special smoky flavor is made. We saw the white oak barrels where the sauce is aged before it's bottled and shipped. It smelled so good in there, but when I tasted some of the hot sauce, I felt like my tongue was on fire! Rosalie made fun of me.

At the factory I learned that both Cajun and Creole cooking use hot pepper sauce. They are both based on French cooking. Uncle Joe says Cajun was country cooking and Creole was New Orleans city food, but they are combined so often these days that they can both be called "South Louisiana Cooking." I don't care what it's called as long as I get to eat it!

Love,
Paul

January 3rd

Dear Mom and Dad,

Today Rosalie and I went to Breaux Bridge, the crawfish capital of the world! I got to learn all about Cajun culture and cuisine.

The original Cajuns were French settlers who showed up in eastern Canada in 1604. When Britain took control of the area, the settlers were forced south and slowly made their way down to Louisiana. In the early years, Cajuns were mostly farmers, trappers, and fishermen, but now they work in all sorts of jobs. The Cajun language is a special kind of French spoken in the parts of Louisiana known as Acadiana. I love the way it sounds.

Louisiana is famous for its spicy Cajun food and music, and Rosalie says that Louisianans really know how to have fun. There's the Jazz Fest in New Orleans, and every September Lafayette holds the Festival Acadiennes, where people can dance to all kinds of music and eat delicious Cajun food.

"Laissez les bon temps rouler!" (Let the good times roll!)

Love,
Paul

On the ninth day of Christmas, my cousin gave to me...

9 Cajun crawfish

8 bottles of hot sauce, 7 secret treasures, 6 ghosts a-spooking,
5 golden horns, 4 riverboats, 3 marsh ducks, 2 baby gators,
and a pelican in a cypress tree.

January 4th

Dear Mom and Dad,

This morning Rosalie sent ten frogs jumping across the breakfast table! She told me we need to start training them for the frog jumping contest at the Rayne Frog Festival next September. Here are the rules my froggies have to follow:

1) They must measure at least four inches from nose to tail and must be bullfrogs, toads, or spring-frogs. 2) All frogs must have a name. 3) You can't feed any hot sauce to your frog to make it jump farther and you definitely can't feed rice to your opponent's frog to slow it down. 4) You can't touch your frog once the race starts, but you can shout at it, blow on it, and jump up and down to cheer it on. 5) Each frog gets only three jumps. 6) There are several races, and the frog that jumps the farthest overall is the winner of the whole festival.

I bet my frogs are going to win!

Love,
Paul

On the tenth day of Christmas,
my cousin gave to me...

10 frogs a-leaping

9 Cajun crawfish,
8 bottles of hot sauce, 7 secret treasures, 6 ghosts a-spooking,
5 golden horns, 4 riverboats, 3 marsh ducks, 2 baby gators,
and a pelican in a cypress tree.

January 5th

Dear Mom and Dad,

Did you know that the honeybee is the state insect of Louisiana? This morning we went to the French Quarter to sample some of that sweet Louisiana honey on our beignets. (They're like puffy donuts without a hole and sometimes are covered with powdered sugar.)

Then Uncle Joe took us fishing in Venice, the last city before the Mississippi River lets out into the Gulf of Mexico. Venice is in Plaquemines Parish. Counties in Louisiana are called parishes. Louisiana is the only state that calls them that!

Our fishing guide took us through the marsh near Venice and said it was the best place to find speckled trout in the winter. He was right! We caught our limit of red fish and trout, and filled Uncle Joe's cooler to the top. When we got home tonight, Uncle Joe cooked our fish on the grill. He promises that in the morning he'll make pancakes for us. I'm going to drown mine in more Louisiana honey.

Love,
Paul

On the eleventh day of Christmas,
my cousin gave to me...

11 bees
a-buzzing

HONEY

10 frogs a-leaping, 9 Cajun crawfish,
8 bottles of hot sauce, 7 secret treasures, 6 ghosts a-spooking,
5 golden horns, 4 riverboats, 3 marsh ducks, 2 baby gators,
and a pelican in a cypress tree.

January 6th

Dear Mom and Dad,

Rosalie gave me twelve strands of the coolest, most sparkly beads to celebrate Twelfth Night—the beginning of Carnival! It sounds like Twelfth Night is as big a celebration as Mardi Gras. I can't wait!

Today is the first day you can buy a King Cake. It's shaped like a puffy wreath with lots of green, gold, and purple icing. Inside every cake is a tiny pink plastic baby. Rosalie got the toy baby in her slice, so it was her turn to buy the next King Cake.

Tonight we're going to see the Phunny Phorty Phellows, a group of friends in costume whose streetcar ride officially starts Carnival each year. They throw the first beads to the crowd, and I'm going to catch some. Rosalie says the magic words are, "Throw me something, mister!"

I'm sad to be leaving tomorrow, but I'll be bringing Carnival home with me!

Love,
Paul

On the twelfth day of Christmas,
my cousin gave to me...

12 strands of sparkles

11 bees a-buzzing, 10 frogs a-leaping, 9 Cajun crawfish,
8 bottles of hot sauce, 7 secret treasures, 6 ghosts a-spooking,
5 golden horns, 4 riverboats, 3 marsh ducks, 2 baby gators,
and a pelican in a cypress tree.

Louisiana: The Pelican State

Capital: Baton Rouge • **State abbreviation:** LA • **State songs:** "You Are My Sunshine" and "Give Me Louisiana" • **State bird:** the brown pelican • **State flower:** the magnolia **State tree:** the bald cypress • **State crustacean:** the crawfish • **State amphibian:** the green tree frog • **Louisiana sports teams:** Saints (football), Zephyrs (baseball), Hornets (basketball)

Some Famous Louisianans:

Geoffrey Beene (1927–2004), born in Haynesville, was an influential clothing designer. Louisiana has proclaimed April 27th "Geoffrey Beene Day."

Terry P. Bradshaw (1948–) was born in Shreveport. A famous football player, personality and sports commentator, he played in the Super Bowl four times with the Pittsburgh Steelers and was twice named their most valuable player.

Michael Ellis DeBakey (1908–) was born in Lake Charles to Lebanese immigrant parents. He is a pioneering heart surgeon and researcher. His inventions have saved the lives of thousands of people.

Ellen Lee DeGeneres (1958–), born in Metairie, is an actress, stand-up comedian, and the Emmy Award-winning host of her own talk show, *The Ellen DeGeneres Show*.

Antoine "Fats" Domino (1928–) was born in New Orleans and has been a music legend since the 1950s, much loved for his boogie-woogie piano style and easygoing, warm vocals. His hits include "Blue Monday" and "Walking to New Orleans."

Paul Prudhomme (1940–), born in Opelousas, is a famous chef known for his Cajun cuisine. He made Cajun cooking world famous.

Norbert Rillieux (1806–1894), inventor, was born in New Orleans. A free man of color educated in Paris, he invented the first triple-effect evaporator. His invention was the greatest contribution to the world's sugar industry and is still used today.

Hurricane Katrina

On August 29, 2005, Hurricane Katrina, a huge and powerful storm, hit the Gulf Coast of the United States, causing great damage, especially in Mississippi and Louisiana. The gigantic storm with its strong winds damaged houses and knocked over ancient trees. In New Orleans, the worst damage came when the storm surge of water broke through the levees that had been built to protect the city. The force of the wind-blown water pushed houses off their foundations as it gushed through the city, flooding 80% of New Orleans. Thousands of people and their pets had to leave their homes; some even died in the flood. Katrina was the most destructive and expensive disaster in the history of the United States. Many residents have come back and are working to rebuild their homes, towns, and cities. Volunteers from all over the country and the world are giving their time and money to help. Scientists are studying what happened during Hurricane Katrina so that cities can plan ahead and keep people safe from future floods and hurricanes.

To New Orleans, then, now and always. —J. C.

With love and gratitude to Shreveport-born drummer Chico Chism, who lived the blues life to the end. —L. A.

Many thanks to our superb researcher, Louisiana storyteller Dianne de Las Casas.

STERLING CHILDREN'S BOOKS
New York
An Imprint of Sterling Publishing
387 Park Avenue South
New York, NY 10016

STERLING CHILDREN'S BOOKS and the distinctive Sterling Children's Books logo are trademarks of Sterling Publishing Co., Inc.

Library of Congress Cataloging-in-Publication Data

Cassels, Jean.
The twelve days of Christmas in Louisiana / Jean Cassels ; illustrated by Lynne Avril.
p. cm.
ISBN-13: 978-1-4027-3814-2
ISBN-10: 1-4027-3814-5
1. Louisiana—Juvenile literature. 2. Counting—Juvenile literature. I. Avril, Lynne, 1951- II. Title.

F369.3.C34 2007
976.3—dc22
2007003951

Lot #:
10 9 8 7 6 5
07/12
Text copyright © 2007 by Sterling Publishing Co., Inc.
Illustrations copyright © 2007 by Lynne Avril
Designed by Jessica Dacher

Distributed in Canada by Sterling Publishing
C/o Canadian Manda Group, 165 Dufferin Street,
Toronto, Ontario, Canada M6K 3H6
Distributed in the United Kingdom by GMC Distribution Services
Castle Place, 166 High Street, Lewes, East Sussex, England BN7 1XU
Distributed in Australia by Capricorn Link (Australia) Pty. Ltd.
P.O. Box 704, Windsor, NSW 2756, Australia

Printed in China
All rights reserved

Sterling ISBN 978-1-4027-3814-2

For information about custom editions, special sales, premium and corporate purchases, please contact Sterling Special Sales Department at 800-805-5489 or specialsales@sterlingpublishing.com.

The artwork was prepared using gouache and colored pencils.

The TABASCO marks, bottle and label designs are registered trademarks and servicemarks exclusively of McIlhenny Company, Avery Island, LA 70513.

Washington
Montana
Oregon
Idaho
Wyoming
Nevada
Utah
Colorado
California
Arizona
New Mexico
Alaska
Hawaii